The EASTER DONKEY

By Isabelle Holland

Illustrated by Judith Cheng

A GOLDEN BOOK • NEW YORK
Western Publishing Company, Inc., Racine, Wisconsin 53404

"Come along, Barak," Seth said to his donkey. "Sophia said we were to get some palm branches."

Barak, who as well as being lame was young and obstinate, went on munching the hay that Seth had brought him earlier, after their return from the market.

"Didn't you hear me?" Seth said. "You can have the rest when we get back."

Barak heard him perfectly well, but he thought he just might get in a couple more mouthfuls of hay before Seth lost his temper and took action. The action would be no more than a slap of Seth's hand on Barak's rump. His rump would not be hurt, but his feelings would be deeply wounded.

"Take a stick to him," Sophia said from the doorway of her small house. "That'll make him move. I need those palm branches by midday. A rich merchant wants all I can give him to spread on the ground for his guests at a banquet tonight, and I don't want anybody else to sell him the palm branches first. So make that beast move. If you don't—" She started forward, picking up a stick.

"He'll move, won't you, Barak?" Seth said anxiously. He knew that if Barak didn't move, Sophia, who had no love for anything or anybody, would come and beat the donkey.

Barak moved, still munching. He had felt the woman's stick when Seth was not there to protect him, and he had no desire to feel it again. When they were at a safe distance, Barak stopped and rubbed his nose against Seth's side, just to show that his occasional stubbornness had nothing to do with his affection for Seth.

"Yes, I know," Seth said, rubbing him in return down his face and between his ears. "She's cruel. But if she doesn't get those branches, she won't pay me, and we won't have anything to eat tonight."

Then they both limped off to see what they could do about
palm branches. Along with the other things that bound them
together, such as having no permanent home and nothing to eat
unless they earned the money to buy it, they were both lame. Seth
had been born that way, and Barak had hurt his leg when his
former owner piled too much on his back, making him stumble
and fall. After that, the owner threw him out of the stable where he
had been born.

No one else would take him in or feed him, and he was
starving outside the city when Seth, in his constant search for
sticks and wood to sell for fuel, found him. Seth himself lived in a
shallow cave just outside the city wall. He managed to get the
donkey to his cave and then brought him food and water and
nursed him until he was better. His leg never completely
straightened, but he grew strong and could move quite rapidly
when he had a mind to. Seth named him Barak, which meant
lightning. They were each other's best friend.

Seth could not remember his father, who had died soon after Seth was born. Seth's mother had taken the best care of him she could while working as a servant in other people's houses. She had not been allowed to keep Seth with her, so she had paid Sophia from her small wages to look after Seth when he was a baby, and she had brought him food from the great houses where she worked. She had been gentle and loving, and Seth had looked forward every day to seeing her.

When his mother died, he thought his heart would break. Sophia told him he could not stay in her house any longer, since his mother was not there to pay her. So he left and slept in doorways and courtyards until he came across the cave he made his home. To earn money for food, he collected sticks and branches for firewood and did errands for some of the men in the bazaar. He did not have many friends. Other children made fun of the lopsided way he walked and occasionally threw stones at him. He was lonely and seldom had enough to eat. Then he found Barak. After that, they were often hungry, but they were not lonely anymore.

Seth had frequently been sent to collect palm branches for one use or another, and he had never had any trouble finding them. He might walk and run in an odd way, but when climbing a tree he was the equal of any boy. But as he looked in the usual places he discovered that many of the trees had been stripped almost bare. "Why is everybody taking palm branches?" he wondered, tired now, and a little afraid that he might not find them in time to be paid. The answer came to him when he looked down out of a tree from which the last few branches had been removed. Far below, he saw a great crowd lining either side of the main road that wound into the city and, on the road itself, covering the surface, branch after branch of palms.

Seth stared at them, while at the foot of the tree Barak munched a few leaves from a small bush.

"How can I get some of those palm branches?" Seth asked himself. He stared down past the roofs of the houses below him. They lined the narrow alleys that wound down the hill on which the city was built. At the top were the Temple, the house of the High Priest, and the palace of the Roman governor. At the bottom were the poorer dwellings.

From his perch Seth tried to see the spot where the crowd lining the road below might be thinnest. He did not like crowds. Sometimes people made fun of him, imitating his jerky walk, and if there was a crowd near, often the rest would take up the jests and the laughter. And he was always afraid of what might happen to Barak if they decided to tease him, too. On the other hand, if he didn't have some palm branches to take back to Sophia, then he and Barak wouldn't eat.

"I'll just have to steal some," Seth told himself.

His mother had taught him that to steal was a violation of the Eighth Commandment—Thou Shalt Not Steal—and was therefore wrong, no matter what the excuse.

But Seth had arrived at a commandment of his own—Thou Shalt Not Go Hungry. And whenever he felt a slight tremor of conscience over disobeying the Law, he reminded himself that as Barak's owner it was his duty to see that his donkey was fed.

"Come along, Barak," he said, shinnying down the tree trunk. "We have to go below."

When they got down to the main road, Seth and Barak worked their way behind the crowd to the place where there were fewer people. Then they crept forward. When they reached the side of the road, Seth understood why he had had such a hard time finding the lower branches on palm trees. Everyone around was holding a palm branch and waving it, and the road itself was almost invisible under the branches laid across it.

"Don't you have a palm branch?" a pleasant voice said beside him.

Seth turned. Standing beside him was a girl of about his own age.

"There weren't any left on the trees that I saw," he said.

"You can have this. I have two," the girl said.

He needed many more than one branch. But so few people had given him something in this way that Seth was embarrassed. "Thank you," he said.

"Here," she said, holding it out. "Take it."

He took the palm branch. The long spiky leaves seemed greener and thicker than most of those around. "Where did you get it?" he asked. He knew that girls did not go up trees to cut off branches, so someone must have given it to her.

"Off a tree," she said. "Only it was easier for me, because the tree was growing just outside the courtyard, and I could get to it quicker than anyone else."

"You mean you climbed up and got it?" Seth asked, astonished.

She grinned. "It was before anyone got up, so I just tied my skirts and went up. If Mother had seen me, she might have scolded, except that she never scolds."

Seth didn't say anything. He was thinking about his mother, who also had never scolded.

"What's your name?" he asked.

"Deborah. What's yours?"

"Seth. And this is Barak." Seth patted Barak on the head.

"What a nice donkey!" She put out her hand and stroked him.

Barak twitched one ear. Normally he didn't like anyone except Seth to touch him. But this girl had a kind voice.

"Why are all the people here?" Seth asked. "Is the governor or the High Priest coming into the city?"

"Haven't you heard? It's Jesus of Nazareth, King of Kings." Deborah stared at Seth's rather blank face. "Don't you know about him?"

Seth shook his head. "I thought Herod was king."

"He's not the real king. This Jesus is. He heals people. He healed old Jacob, who sat at the gate—you know, the one who'd been there for years, all bent and crippled."

Now, Seth knew who Jacob was, and suddenly he realized that of late he hadn't seen the aged cripple seated in his usual place, his legs twisted under him, begging for alms.

"You say this Jesus healed him?"

"He just said, 'Rise!' and Jacob slowly started moving his legs. Everybody who saw it said they could see the legs filling out, like they were normal, and then he stood up, and it was as though he'd never been crippled."

"Did you see it?" Seth asked.

"No."

"Oh."

"But I did see him heal a blind man."

"You actually *saw* it?"

"Yes. He spat on the man's eyes and put his hands on them and asked if he could see anything. And the man said yes, he could see men, like trees, walking. Then Jesus put his hands again on the man's eyes and told him to look up. And the man could see everything. Mother and I were standing near, and we saw it all."

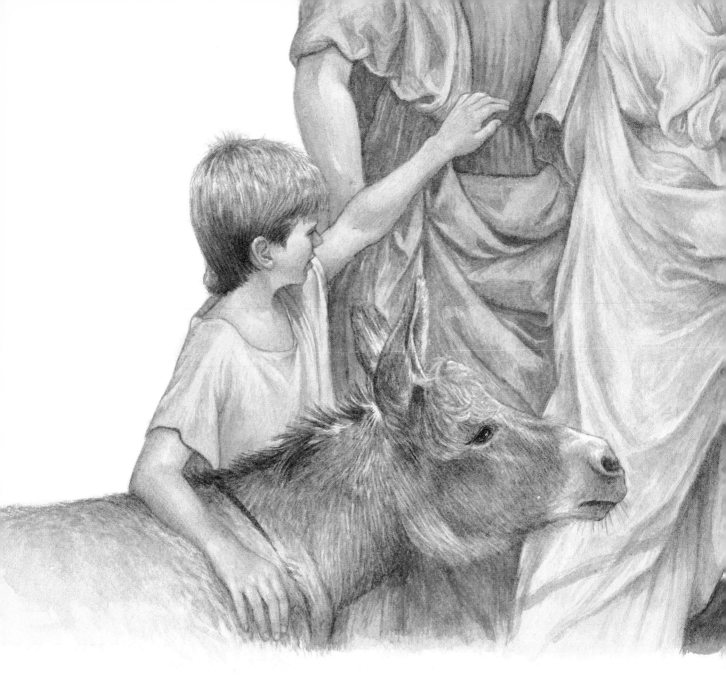

Seth looked into Deborah's brown eyes and found that, with all his experience in people lying and telling half-truths, he could not doubt her. Then, without thinking, he looked at Barak's leg and then at his own. "Would he heal us, do you think?"

"Ask him, when he comes riding by. He's supposed to be here any time now."

Seth pulled Barak in line. He could hear the shouts and the hosannas from down the road. "Hail, hail!" the crowd cried. "Hail!"

"Hail!" Seth cried, even though he couldn't see anything at the moment. The people beside him blocked his view. But his heart was beating. With one hand he clung to Barak, and then he slid his arm around the donkey's neck.

"We'll be well, Barak. We'll be able to walk. Then we can get better jobs and earn some money and have good food and everything...HAIL!" he called out and then opened his mouth to shout the word again. But nothing came out.

The man riding by on a donkey had a face that struck Seth like a light, although later he couldn't have described it in detail.

"Please!" he heard himself cry out. "Please! Heal Barak. Make his leg well. Please make his leg well!" Under his hand he could feel the donkey tremble.

The man looked at him and at the donkey, and, for a moment, he smiled. Then he passed on, and the crowd closed in around his back.

Seth, Deborah, and Barak stood there as people flocked after the man on the donkey. After a minute, Seth looked at his leg. It was as out of shape as ever. "Barak," he said gently. "Come, take a step."

Barak hobbled forward a step or two. He, too, was as lame as he had been.

Disappointment and anger rushed through Seth. "It's a lie, Deborah. You couldn't have seen him heal the blind man. It's just foolish talk, and you were stupid enough to believe it." He was furious with Deborah because he was furious with the man on the donkey, who hadn't healed either him or Barak. But the man was gone, and Deborah was standing there.

"I am not stupid. I saw it. I don't know why he didn't heal you, but he *did* heal the blind man and he *did* heal Jacob."

Seth was a little ashamed of his outburst against Deborah. After all, she had given him the palm branch. That reminded him of why he and Barak were there. Leaning down, he started quickly picking up some of the palm branches from the street.

"Just what do you think you're doing?" a man's voice said. "Those palm branches are ours. We picked them, and we're going to sell them. Hand them over."

But an angry, stubborn streak had seized Seth. He clung to the branches he already had and stooped to pick one more.

"Out of the way!" the man said. He picked Seth up as though he were a fly, tore the branches from his arms, and then punched him. "Thief!" he said. "Do you know what they do to thieves where I come from? They stone them!" He turned. "Is this your donkey? Well, they'd stone him, too!" And he shoved poor Barak and then brought his belt down across the donkey's back. "I suppose you stole those branches the beast is carrying! Well, I'll take those, too!" He pulled the baskets on Barak's back. Barak gave a wild bray, because the strap holding the baskets was almost cutting him in two.

"Leave him alone!" Seth cried. He launched himself against the man.

The man laughed in an ugly way. "Behold the midget, the cripple!" He picked up Seth and held him over his head.

Deborah screamed. Barak brayed again. Somehow Seth wiggled free and jumped to the ground. Then Barak lowered his head and butted the man in the back.

"Oof!" the man said as the air went out of him. Abruptly he sat down.

"Barak, let's go," Seth said. The man's friends were beginning to gather.

"Where do you think you're going?" one of the men asked, standing in front of Seth and Barak.

"Leave him be at once," an imperious voice said.

They all turned. Deborah, looking and sounding not like the little girl who had given Seth his palm branch but like a haughty aristocrat, went on. "This boy is employed by my mother, who is a member of the High Priest's household. You lay one finger on him or his donkey, and the soldiers will come and drive you from the bazaar."

There was a moment of silence. Deborah stood straight, looking as though she had spent her young life commanding people. Seth and Barak waited, not daring to breathe.

Then Deborah turned. "You can come with me now," she said to Seth and Barak, "and bring those palm branches with you. The High Priest's household has need of them."

Seth did not like to be ordered about, not even by somebody who had helped him out. But his own and Barak's safety came first. So, after piling many more of the branches into Barak's baskets, he followed Deborah up the road, aware of the eyes that were on him.

When they were out of sight of the men, Deborah turned to Seth. "I'm sorry I ordered you about like that, but it was the only way I could be sure they'd leave you alone."

"It's all right," Seth said. "Thank you for helping us." He shivered, remembering the scene and the ugly faces and the strap coming down on Barak's back. Seth couldn't bear to think what might happen to Barak if they were separated. With his bad leg, poor Barak couldn't run really fast, and men like that could be cruel. "Thank you," he said again, and he put his hand on Barak's neck.

Deborah rubbed Barak between the ears. "I can see he's special," she said.

"Does your mother really work in the High Priest's household?" Seth asked. He'd never met anyone who came from such an exalted background.

"Yes." Then she burst out, "I'm worried about what they're going to do to Jesus of Nazareth. Some of the rulers of the household are angry with him, and I'm sure they're plotting something."

Seth felt his own anger with this Jesus. If he could heal a lame man, why couldn't he heal a lame donkey, especially since the donkey was always in danger from rough people who would abuse him? "He didn't heal Barak," he said.

"No." Deborah hesitated. "Perhaps there was a reason—a reason you can't know."

Seth, still angry, said nothing.

When they reached the courtyard of the High Priest's house, Seth stopped, overawed by the size and splendor of the place. There were people everywhere, many of them richly dressed. Even the servants looked well cared for and well fed. Seth noticed that some of those on the High Priest's staff were standing near the gate, carrying swords.

"Who's this?" one of them asked Deborah.

"He's bringing some wood and palm branches to my mother. She ordered them."

"From this urchin? Isaac from the bazaar usually brings your mother's wood." The man looked down at Barak's lame leg. "At least Isaac has strong donkeys."

"Barak's very strong," Seth said angrily. "He's also very intelligent."

"I'll bet," the man said. "Let's see how fast his reactions are!" He drew back his leg.

"No!" Seth cried and flung himself in front of Barak, getting the soldier's foot in his side.

"Now look what you've done!" Deborah said angrily.

A tall woman who looked very much like Deborah approached. "What is all this fuss about?"

The guard, Seth, and Deborah all talked at once.

"Quiet!" the woman said, but she was smiling. For a moment she looked at Seth and Barak. Then she said to the soldier, "I don't know what your problem is with this boy. I asked him to bring me some palm branches, which I see he's done."

"But I thought Isaac was the one you bought branches from," the guard said.

"I buy branches from whomever it suits me," the woman replied. Then she turned to Seth. "Thank you for bringing the wood. Here is your pay."

Seth took it. "Thank you," he said. He was afraid to look at what she had put in his hand, but he was sure it was more than he had ever been paid. He and Barak would have food now.

That was the only good thing that happened that week.
Everything seemed to get worse. The whole city was restless.
Knots of people stood around arguing angrily. And anger like that,
Seth knew from unhappy experience, often spilled out onto him
and Barak. Sticks and branches were hard to find, and when he
and Barak did gather some, they were stolen from them. Watching
Barak walking painfully after two bullies had taken the wood in
his baskets and then kicked him, Seth's anger at Jesus for not
healing Barak grew.

And the angrier he got, the more he and Barak seemed to run
into trouble.

"It's not fair," Seth said furiously. "He should have healed you." And he gave Barak an extra wisp of hay that he had stolen from a merchant's stable, where he had brought some wood.

Wednesday night he and Barak went to bed hungry.

Thursday they awoke weary and even hungrier, and they had their first basket of wood and branches stolen on the way to the market.

By nightfall they still had not been paid for anything and had not eaten.

"Perhaps," Seth thought, "if we could get a few more branches, we could take them up to the High Priest's house, and Deborah or her mother would buy them."

Weary as they both were, they managed to collect a few more branches.

It was a long climb, and it was very late. Both Seth and Barak were tired when they reached the big gates of the High Priest's house. But Seth could see right away that no one was in the frame of mind to buy anything. Torches were lit in the courtyard. From inside the house came the sound of raucous laughter. Most of the guards had left the gate and were crowded around the door through which the laughter was coming.

"What's happening?" Seth whispered to the single guard left standing near the gate.

"It's Jesus of Nazareth, the miracle worker," the guard sneered. "He isn't much of a miracle worker if he can't get himself out of that."

Feeling Barak trembling with fatigue under his hand, Seth knew a jab of angry pleasure. This Jesus had not helped Barak. He deserved whatever was being done to him. "What are they doing?" he asked.

"Oh, just having a bit of fun. Go on up there, if you want to. I'll watch your donkey."

Seth knew he shouldn't leave Barak. But his anger was so great that he forgot. He wanted to see the impostor punished.

"I'll be back," he said to Barak.

The last thing he heard as he ran forward was Barak's plaintive bray of protest and fear.

The man was standing in a circle of laughing, jeering people in the great hall of the High Priest's house. Some of them were spitting into his face. Others hit him. One man yelled between buffeting blows, "If you're a prophet, prophesy! Say who hit you!"

There was a roar of laughter.

"Yes," Seth, who was watching near the door, thought angrily. "And if you're a healer, why don't you heal?" His fury at Jesus for not healing Barak and himself grew as he watched the cruel ridicule. And as it grew, his anger pushed down a very different feeling that he refused even to look at.

At that moment a big man who had been standing nearby, arguing with a servant, suddenly yelled, "I tell you, I don't know who this Jesus is! I never heard of him!" And with that the man shoved his way out of the courtyard.

For a moment the yelling and jeers and laughter seemed to pause. There was a moment's eerie stillness. Then the silence was pierced by an unexpected sound—the crowing of a cock.

Seth shivered. Suddenly he hated everything about the scene. "It will be dawn soon," he thought. At that moment he remembered he had left Barak at the gate. Fear streaked through him. "Barak!" he yelled, running to the gate. "Barak!"

But Barak wasn't there. Nor was he anywhere else in the courtyard.

Weary and frightened, grief tearing at his heart, Seth looked down every street and searched every courtyard. He asked everyone he met if they had seen a small lame donkey. Most of the people just laughed at him. A few cuffed him. His own lame leg gave way several times, and he fell, bruising himself.

"It's that Jesus' fault for not healing Barak," he told himself. "If he had just healed him, I wouldn't have left him at the gate."

He told himself this again and again, to make sure the anger didn't go away. He had a painful suspicion that if the anger went, something far worse would take its place. So, as he searched the streets and courtyards, calling Barak's name, he kept reminding himself that it was all Jesus' fault, not only that Barak wasn't healed but that he was now lost. Seth had somehow managed to cut his good foot, so he was even more lame than before. But though it hurt to run, he moved as fast as he could, trying not to think of what might have happened to Barak.

It was now daylight, and the streets were filled with people whispering, crying, or shouting with anger. Trying to dodge around them, asking anyone who looked as though he might answer if he had seen Barak, Seth ran into whole crowds who appeared to be watching something go along the road. But Seth was too short to see over them. Once he asked someone in the crowd what he was watching.

"Just a criminal being led off to be crucified," the man said.

It seemed a long time later when he almost stumbled against a girl sitting on a doorstep, crying. A second look told him it was Deborah.

"Barak's lost," he said. "Have you seen him?"

"No," Deborah replied. "They've taken Jesus," she said. "They're going to kill him."

"If it wasn't for him, Barak wouldn't be lost!"

Deborah straightened. "What did you say?"

Seth reminded himself of how angry he was. "I only left Barak a minute to see what was happening in the High Priest's house. But when I went back to the gate, Barak was gone."

"You left Barak with that mob?"

The terrible feeling that had been threatening to overcome Seth now pushed its way nearer to the surface. Seth's anger against Jesus made a last stand. "It wasn't my fault. If he'd just healed Barak—"

"You left Barak by himself with those people just to see them torment Jesus? And you say it's Jesus' fault that Barak is lost?"

In the early morning light, Seth could see Deborah's expression, and he wished he couldn't. He could have borne the anger in her eyes. What he could not bear was the shame that now filled him as she looked at him. And he realized that it was shame that had been pushing at him all the hours he had been searching the streets for Barak.

With a cry, he turned and ran. But he could no longer outrun the knowledge that losing Barak was his own fault. If he had not yielded to the ugly impulse to join the mocking crowd around Jesus, Barak would still be with him. When Seth tried to imagine what could happen to a small, young, frightened, lame donkey at the hands of brutal and angry men, he felt his heart break.

Many hours later, having searched everywhere else, he came to a barren field on a hill outside the city. It was an eerie, frightening place, and Seth remembered that it was called Golgotha, or the Place of the Skull.

As he crept forward he saw the crosses, three of them, and he shivered. It was well known that the Romans executed their criminals on crosses. Seth wondered which poor man had run afoul of the Roman occupier. Then, as he stared, he recognized the man nailed by his feet and hands to the middle cross. Since Seth had seen Jesus in the High Priest's house, someone had put a circle of thorns on his head.

So they had finally killed poor Jesus, after tormenting him. Seth crept forward. There were only a few people around the cross now—two women, a young man, and a Roman centurion.

Seth stared up at the face that had looked like a light when Seth first saw it.

His own sense of shame swept over him like a wave. He was sure that somehow his anger, his eagerness to blame Jesus for Barak's being lost, had helped bring this man to his awful death.

"I'm sorry," he whispered. "I'm sorry."

Seth put his face down on the earth and cried. "I'm sorry," he whispered again. "Truly."

It was many hours later when Seth awoke. He looked around, not knowing where he was or how he got there. Then memory came back. First he remembered that Barak was lost. Then he remembered the man on the cross. The cross was empty now. The other two crosses still held their dead victims, but Jesus was gone. Then Seth remembered why Barak was gone, and his heart filled again with misery and loneliness and shame.

Slowly Seth got up. He was so bruised that he could hardly move, and the first time he put any weight on his bad leg, he stumbled and fell.

"Barak's lost." The words kept rhythm as he limped back toward his cave. It was so long since he had eaten that he wasn't even hungry. But he was weak, and he knew that if he didn't get something to eat, he would fall and not get up.

He was about halfway home when someone tossed some bread out of a kitchen door. Seth fell on it and choked it down. When the woman came to the door to throw something else out, she saw him. She took pity on Seth and gave him goat's milk as well.

"There are people who are kind," he thought, drinking thirstily. And he prayed that somehow Barak had met them.

Finally his cave came in sight. With the last of his strength he climbed up to it and then stopped. There, looking as anxious as Seth had been, was Barak.

Barak gave a loud bray of joy and struggled to his feet. Seth ran and flung his arms around his neck. "Thank you," he whispered, and he realized that he was addressing the man who had been on the cross. "Thank you!"

For the remainder of that day and the next, Seth and Barak rested, only venturing out for any scraps of food they could find.

The day after that, the first day of the week, they started out again to gather some wood and branches. The wood was as scarce as usual, and both of them moved more slowly because of their ordeal. But it didn't matter. They were happy to be together.

In the middle of the day, when they were on the road into the city, a man suddenly appeared in front of them.

Seth stared, not believing what he saw. Jesus was dead. He had been tormented and nailed to a cross and killed. How could he be standing there?

"Barak," Seth whispered, "do you see what I do?" He could feel Barak quivering under his hand.

The man came and stood near them. He smiled and touched them both. Then he was gone. Seth tried to see what happened to him, but a light was blinding his eyes.

Happiness surged through Seth, and then fiery pain. His lame leg felt as though lightning bolts were going through it, as though a giant hand were reshaping it. Dazed, faintly aware that Barak for some reason was making a fearful noise with his braying, Seth stepped forward hesitantly, dipping down on one side as he always did to allow for his short leg. Then he nearly fell flat, because the ground seemed to come up and hit his foot. He caught himself and then stared down. His brown dusty legs were exactly the same and both strong.

"Barak!" he yelled. "Barak, I'm not lame!" He stared around, trying to find Jesus again. But there was no one there. Only the air itself seemed tinged with a golden light.

"Barak, Barak!" He had to yell, because the little donkey was running around and around, kicking up his heels and braying with delight as his four perfect legs carried him as swiftly as any other donkey.

"Barak, oh, Barak!" Seth leaned down and hugged his friend. "We're healed," he whispered. "He forgave me and we're healed!"

Then he said, "We must go and show Deborah. We have to tell her that we've seen the Lord and we are healed."